Dear Someone

BookSquirrel Publications

BookSquirrel Publication

Mahadev Totala Nager, Indore (M.P),452001

Regd Under MSME

Website:

www.booksquirrelpublication.com

"Dear Someone"

By: Rubal Choudhary and Ishani Agarwal

ISBN: 978-93-89923-58-2

English Anthology

Book Formatting: Rubal Choudhary

Cover Design: Ronak Chavda

Disclaimer

This Anthology is a work of fiction. The writers have tried to make sure that all the Write-ups in this book are original, and plagiarism free.

All the write-ups in this book are unique, and they belong solely to the Co-Authors.

In case of any detection of Plagiarism, neither the publishing house, nor the compiler is to be held responsible.

The sole responsibilities of the Write-ups are on that writer

Acknowledgement

The making of this Anthology would not have been possible without the co-authors. A gratitude towards all who have worked hard and have made effort for this book to be a success.

I am thankful to BookSquirrel Publications without whom this project would not be possible.

Above all, the hearthy thanks to our parents, family and friends for supporting us throughout this project. Lastly, we thank the almighty for giving us this opportunity and strength to complete it successfully.

Well hey!

I know letters are not my type of writing, and you also know that very well so just follow up, and don't get left behind.

So it has been a very long since we have been Apart.
And so much have changed in the meantime…
Like first of talking about us
We have changed so much that we not even know we are the same or not…
If say for myself well things are turning out good in life now,
Am getting the respect I always dreamed about!

You know the happiness I Always told you I want, Am actually getting it now, but I don't feel that great
Like its Incomplete....

Guess it's your absence!

Well never mind that, you know na am an Emotional Hag!
Now I handle Situation more efficiently and I don't sit and cry in it like I used too!
But yeah I still try to walk road with someone or other
Am still not a fan to walk alone as before….
So I get a left alone very often by friends yea I don't make any as close as you….
By the way am used to this now!
So yea it's okay for me….
Seeking for new people and then getting separate is a open thing now,
But am happy the way life is going on, hoping for beat for work ……
and us
Aaaa…
Guess it's now long
So I will just close it off!

Just want to let you know
That
Am happy and perfect and also ready to try out things again and better
…
Will you? I don't need an answer its okay!
Signing out

Yours
Idiot

Ashutosh Das

Hey Mr Special

I know it's not been so long we have been known to each other, but the feeling of attachment and care has been started.

Everything you do for me is to keep me happy no matter what the situation is.So starting from the very first day, you were a person whom I talked and I felt like a friend in one go, which is for most not easy , but for me it was altogether a different feeling.

You have given me things what I have never expected from a friend.Ya I know we are not just friends, we are more than that, that is why we call each other SPECIAL.

I know it's a very strong word and I mean it.Not even a single day has passed when you have not treated me like a baby with full of care and protectiveness.

I must say You are GEM of a PERSON, (I know it's all because of me, what you call it in Hindi - Sangati ka Asar).Knowing you from the very first day to till now, you, your nature, your care and love towards me have remained constant.And I always wanted a friend, who can keep himself constant through our relationship.

Coming on to our Bond, I really cannot express it, bcz it's way beyond Special and beautiful. I just pray that we last long together to make our goals happen and achieve whatever we have wished to.

Goal- A word which define our aiming right, and yes we too have made goals and that to alot, not just the craziest ones but emotional ones too.

From your wishing me in the morning at first to saying 11:11 stay forever at night, it's just have become my favorite thing and I want to read this forever from your side.

Everyone makes goal (Friendship Goals u call it) of having- same clothes, taking selfies, having stuffs, but your goals are the bestest so far.

When you said me to have me in your arms and traveling to a South Temple, it made me cry because that is what I never expected from anyone.And yes as you said in the starting, unexpected things are the best, so as our relationship.

It holded true in our case.

From calling me jaani, Bacha, dumbo when I am happy to being with me when I am crying,

You owned it.You really owned it!

Let me now thank you for some very Important things-

Thank you for making me feel Happy all the times.

Thank you for making my low mood to boost up

Thank you for making me realise that I m wrong sometimes

Thank you for always showing concern and care towards me.

Thank you for bearing me every time

Thank you for making me one of your priorities.

Thank you for adding me in your Pin chats.

Lastly, Thank you for having me with you.

I have a hell lot of things to say but I think I should stop here bcz I don't want you to reach on cloud 9 because , it would not be easy for me to make you normal. (Hehe)

I miss you

Yours –

Rubal Choudhary

Dear You..

Yes, it is you I am talking about.

For others, you are a mystery. But when you read this letter, you will understand for sure.

Well, I doubt if this letter will ever reach you.

It started so suddenly. We started talking, and then, we got close. You proposed, and I said Yes.

I know I was a fool. Who says yes in just 5 days of knowing a stranger? But then, I had my defenses ready. I was in Love. A Love like none other.

In the beginning, I felt as if my life was set. The perfect mix of attention and care you were. But as time went by, you started getting busy with work. I did not complain, coz I understood work is important. But still, you took out time for me on weekends to Meet. I would wait for night to come, so that I got to talk to you.

But with time, everything changed. We fought and broke up. And you did not bother talking to me for 2 months. Then one fine day, when I was on the verge of letting you go from my heart, you came back. Again like a fool, I accepted all your apologies, and forgave you.

Again, a bit dismissive I was in the beginning, but with time, I started being the old me again. I started thinking of a future with you. And you did it again.

A fight for no reason whatsoever. Again the same routine followed. Breakup, and then you keeping no contact. The only difference was, this Time, it took you 4 months to get back.

And then ? Well, I was a fool no more.

I have let you go now.

Yes, it still hurts at times, but I am happy.

Dear you, always remember, play once, and you can be forgiven, but again ? Well.. Not a fool all the time.

Not yours anymore,

Someone, who knew you in and out .

Ishani Agarwal

<u>C0- Authors</u>

1) Akash Maliya
2) Ananya Srivastava
3) Anjana Agarwal
4) Anonymous
5) Aryansh Arora
6) Astha Yadav
7) Ayesha Shaikh
8) Bhaskar Malakar
9) Danica Rayen
10) Darshna Suraj
11) Deep Thind
12) Dipika Gouda
13) Dr Tilak Dixit
14) Gargi Chatterjee
15) Harpreet Kaur
16) Ishika Agarwal
17) Ishika Agrawal
18) Jaishi Jaiswal
19) Jiaul Islam
20) Lakshita Srimali
21) Mahalakshmi Harsha
22) Mamta Bhagat
23) Md. Sohail Rafiq
24) Mohit Birla
25) MuskanBaheti
26) Muskan Sachdeva
27) Nishant Vaidya
28) Pardeep Bogra
29) Pavani Vedantham
30) Pawan Pratap Singh
31) Payal Banerjee
32) Poorvi Kumar

33) Pratyasha Chakraborty
34) Prem Kumar
35) Rahul Tamang
36) Riya Rashmi Dash
37) Riyanshi Gupta
38) Sakshi Agrawal
39) Samriddhi Jaiswal
40) Sanjukta Raychaudhuri
41) SayaliWadke
42) Shubham Shah
43) Sreshtha Das
44) Suchismita Ghoshal
45) Surya
46) Sushil Kumar Gocchhayat
47) Sushmita Shaw
48) Swarnalata Behera
49) SwarupaGhatak
50) Vaishali Goel

Dearest ____,
I've always struggled to tell you something but never got the chance to say it or more like I was never able to muster the courage to tell you. Its peculiar of me to think that you'll understand on your own. Moreover, how am I supposed to tell you that the moment I see you, I grow oblivious to the world around me? When the air lightly brushes your hair off your face, I fall deep into a different universe. I watch you when you're not looking, and adore you when you aren't even aware of it. While awake, I keep my mind busy with your daydreams. I want to tell you that I love walking in the rain with you, I love eating ice cream with my chattering teeth during winters if its with you, I love sitting in the canteen with you and drinking tea and I love having all those late night conversations when we talk about all the things that we did together all day but how should I say this to you? Yes, I know I'm your bestfriend and you share every single thing with me, I know you don't want to lose me and neither do I ever want to spend any day of my life without your presence in it. You're so precious to me and maybe that's the reason why I've never been able to say all this to you. I'm too scared to be left by you, too scared to not have these precious days with you. Even today, this is going to just be a page in my diary, in which I've expressed all my love for you so many times before, in a hope that, one day you'll understand on your own.

You're priceless to me,
a feeling for me.
No matter how you are,
you're near to me.

Your bestfriend,
Akash Maliya

Akash Maliya...

Hey

The day I have seen you at the road was not a good feeling but from that day you just become a addiction of mine,
I dont know its true love or infatuation but it was something and their was a little bond b/w us which makes me curious to have a look of you !
As everyone knows ,a vehicle without petrol oil is waste and the same the relationship without love is worst a relationship is like a seesaw you both have to put same efforts but i was little confuse that we have same feelings or only i have ?????
Sometime that one sided love makes me scared of loosing you but its okay i'll love you at any cost no matter who comes in my life!! finally that day comes when we get a chance to be together and day passes and now we are separated but my feelings for you is still constant......
I hope we will meet at some point of life but cant stay together as we were in the past and you are still unaware from some feelings of mine but I just wants to tell you that you are the sunshine of my life.

No matter rain comes or go it have to rise everyday .

I have never cheated on you it was the misunderstanding which was created by our ego but i just wants to say you that again i wants to be in your arm like I was, again I wants to let you play with my hairs as you had ,again I have to behave like a kid like i was, again i wants to hear your unwanted talks, again i want to love the way you breathe, a single day thinking about you is not possible and idont even think I know now you have created your own world but what about me ....????
Still I am waiting for you, everyday when the door bellrangs, you are the one who comes in my mind and I'll wait for you and

I will forever

You're beloved
Ananya!

Ananya Srivastava

Dear God,

You made this universe. Now, you have started giving people this virus. Why did you do it? Is the world full of sin now? Or is it that you want population under control?
If it is sin, then the sinner is not actually getting punished. It is the innocent being attacked more. And if population, then that is your giving. Why make us suffer?
My thinking is, if sin increases, put the sinner to suffer, nit the innocent. It is unbearable to see small children suffer. Be it rape, or any other kind of illness, small kids are also suffering every day. If you want to decrease population, why make kids? You can make all parents impotent, so they don't have kids.
If you have given us life, you should let us live. Not make us suffer throughout.
For females, it is impossible to Even move out safely now a days. Please give us a way out of it. If you think removing females altogether helps, then do that. Of not, please save them.
It is a request dear God, please remove this virus. Let us live.
Being a female, I am expressing my heart out to you.
Thank you God if you hear me.

Your Loving Daughter.

Anjana Agarwal

Dear A

For the very first time I am finding it difficult to start a letter addressed to you. Writing a letter to you came very easy for me I just had to grab a pen and start pouring my heart out. But now I am doing this after nine years. FYI I can't stop smiling over my stupidity of doing this.

In this age of social media I don't know anything about you. So I am writing this anonymous letter to you in a little hope that you will find it in a corner of a book store.

Let me start it this way by apologising for the hundredth time. I know you have forgiven me. I know that you never hated me for all that I have done to you. But it's me; I am unable to forgive myself. I still live in the guilt of leaving you and spoiling your career. To be honest I actually spoiled my life after breaking up with you. I thought that you are the one who is creating problems in my life and making it complicated. The irony was that I was the safest when I was with you. I wanted to be free in life and also hated the part of being answerable to anyone. Today when I look back I feel no respect for myself. I destroyed my life completely. Remember I gave you the excuse that I don't want to spoil my reputation in school for being with a guy. But my reputation was spoiled after I left you. I got involved in so many nuisance which created disasters in my life. I don't know how you handled the news of my relationships with other guys. You tried so hard to stop me; you were the one standing by me always. But the stupid girl inside me was just running away from you (my happiness). You were right I was not a girl who could manage two cell phones. I always needed a person in my life to keep me on track. It was better when you were doing this task.

I was influenced by all my friends to leave you. No one was supporting me then. I don't know how ethically right or wrong I was. If not then but eventually we would have surely broken up. We were poles apart.

Do you miss me? Do your friends still take my name to tease you at

times?
When you see a younger couple does it ring a bell?
I will tell you what happens with me. None of friend takes your name. You don't even show up at any mutual platforms. When someone mentions first love I go on a roller coaster ride of memories. Everyone was right; people never forget their first love. It also reminds me of the fact that I was not your first.
Coming to the happy times I miss them all yaar. Just few days back I was narrating my cousin how you proposed me in standard eight. It was a start of something very beautiful of my life. I remember how we used to pass letters. Those few lines of your first letter are still stuck in my heart. The dates we went on were not actually dates but it was cute.
I don't know if I have ever mentioned this to you. But today if I can write or proudly call myself a writer it is all because of you. You made me write letters; which helped me to play with words. You have always helped me in my life.
I won't say that I still love you but I do miss you.
You still bring a smile on my face.
Thank you for being there always.

Shona

Anonymous

Hey Aryan ,

How are you ? First of all congratulations now you are going good .You are now a record holder,your first book is coming soon and you have a good company now.So congratulations for that.I am happy for you but it looks like you are not happy for yourself.

I know that your biggest problem is your past.You are always afraid of the fact that some people will come from your past and will ruin your present and future.Dont think about them.Enjoy these days.They will not come now, infact forever.Now they all are gone and now you should move on as well.And if they come ,now you are not alone.On 25th january 2018 you were alone and they took the opportunity.Its 2020 , you have an army now and no one can do anything now.

So now just remember something,don't get possessive , insecure and don't hide things.Being insecure is useless because what's written in the fate,its final.Even you can't change it.If someone is planning to betray you ,don't wait for their chance.Just live your life and ups and downs will come, specially in your case because you have a lot to do in life.

Yours,

The friend whom you saw today in mirror.

Aryansh Arora

I still remember the day when we went to watch the movie, you were watching the movie and I was watching you.Maybe You've forgotten.But I remember well.

I still remember when we were feeding each other popcorn with our hands and your cold drinks accidentally fell and you had scream.

maybe You've forgotten.
But i remember well.

I remember when your head was on my chest and I was stroking your hair with my hands and I kissed your forehead and gently told you I love you and you told me very slowly with smile I love you too.

maybe You've forgotten.
But i remember well.

I remember when your hair was shattered while watching the movie, I did fixed your hair with my hands.

maybe You've forgotten.
But i remember well.

I remember when we was leaving the theater, I hugged you tightly and said to you be with me forever, never forget me.

maybe You've forgotten.
But i remember well.

Dear someone,

I know you are depressed,
I know you are fed up of these ups and downs of life,
I know you are fed up of being sad all the time,
But these are not the reasons to end your precious life.
I know you feel like no one loves you, You feel bullied when
someone comments on your physical appearance,
I know you feel useless sometimes,
But these are not the reasons to finish your life at once.

Life is not about being a winner every time, Life is not about being
loved by everyone who is a part of your life, Life is absolutely not
about caring what others think of you.

Life is just not messy, it is beautiful, Just close your eyes and feel
your inner conscience, just look up at that blue sky, look at the
beautiful city lights during the night time, look at the moon and
stars up there in the sky, look that shine in your parents eyes which
are filled with pride to have you as their child.
Life is worth more than caring about people's opinions,
it is all about learning from the mistakes, about pampering yourself,
discovering yourself and most importantly about loving yourself the
way you are!

Sincerely,
Your Beautiful life.

Astha Yadav

Dear Someone,

I hope this letter finds you well, and I hope that life has treated you kind after all these years. You wrote a letter to me about fifteen years ago, but I still couldn't find the courage in me to write you back. I know how overwhelmed you must feel, reading these words, and I know you're probably wondering why I decided to contact you after all these years. You must have a list of questions you probably want to ask me. Don't worry, and I will answer each one of them soon.

Do you remember the day we met? You were stealing mangoes from the nearby stall when I saw you, but I didn't tell that to anyone. In the end, you and I both shared the mangoes and ate as much as we could. From that day onward, I knew that we were going to be incredible friends. The days spent in Hindustan are blurry, my memories are getting hazy by the day. I've forgotten the sound of your voice and I don't remember every moment that I've spent with you. After all, we were only sixteen when we were separated from each other. When my parents got me into a school, you convinced your family to let you study too. Barefoot, we'd walk to school. And on our way back, we'd play with marbles and stones. Those were simpler days, weren't they? The children of this generation don't know the enjoyment of playing in the mud or dancing in the rain until we got a high fever. And as we grew taller, we'd climb the biggest tree of our town and peek at all of the houses below.

I remember you once told me that you wanted to live in a house as big as those British owned. You envied their lifestyle; you envied the power they had over people like us. I hope you got everything that you've dreamt of. With this letter is a picture attached. Do you remember this day? When one of your elder sisters got married, and we'd watch the bride excitedly, hoping that we'd dress up like this one day too. Your mother painted my hands and feet with henna. Laughing our hearts out, with sparkling eyes and a happy heart, never knew we'd end up like this separated in different countries that seem to be rivals just because of politics. However, I still believe that despite everything, people are always good at heart which no one recognizes, wish we could read hearts.

After one month of your sister's wedding, she and her husband both got killed in a rally. People always asked me why a Muslim girl like me would befriend someone from Hindustan? But they don't know, love, care, and which doesn't see the color of one's skin. I was too young to pay any heed to anything they'd say against. It angered me to see the way this world worked. So much hatred, and what for? All I knew was that being with you made me feel alive. If I am honest, after all these years, I've never felt as happy as I've felt with you. Sure, I made a lot of beautiful memories. But, none of them compared to the ones I've made with you. If I could buy a time machine, I would. If I could go back in time and tell you that you were not only a friend, you were a sister; I would. But I guess it's never too late to express how we truly feel and I'm sure you felt the same way also. When we got separated, I secretly hoped that you had arrived on the train with me too. Years later, wherever I went, I kept searching for you.

A part of me yearned for you. We had the kind of friendship that happens only once in a lifetime, and I lost you. What could we have done? If it were up to me, I would've come to India to meet you fifteen years ago when you wrote that letter to me. But we're helpless against the way this world works, dear. I'm sure; you would've done the same too. A lot of events had occurred in these past few years. But if I start writing, it might take me a thousand pages more. A lot of things had happened in these past few years. My parents got separated from me too on the night of 14th August 1947. I have no idea where they went nor do I know if they're even alive. A family took me in as their house worker. With little money that I earned, I completed my degree in BA and started my job as a teacher in a girls' school. I met a good man who owned his very own business of artifacts and historical sculptures. I gave birth to two beautiful girls, and I named one after you. We got married in a small intimate gathering. In my every moment of happiness and sadness, I thought of you. I wondered where you were, how you had been doing.

In all these years, I have always sent you many presents and letters which didn't reach your way. I understand, no tears, but I miss you. My bones are starting to weaken, and my entire body aches now. There are days when I can't even get out of bed, and there are days when I sleep for fifteen hours. Nights are getting lonelier and the days are getting longer. But I guess that's what happens when you grow older. Everything starts to seem a bit duller and you wonder when this misery will end. If there ever comes a day when the tensions lessen, when you and I can finally visit each other's countries, I hope I stay alive to see that day and I hope you do too. Until we meet again, I hope you know how much I genuinely love you.

Your soul sister always,

And a friend across the borders.

Ayesha Shaikh 

Dear one,

Often for the less of hatred and more inclined towards red hate, which I would refer as the love that still I feel.Kind of love what I pioneer too yet it ain't that love we used to share. Never have I ever even in last bye thought this was the last one. Now my life and your left vive are always there in the mean time of this crucial turn over. Definitely I lost you whenever got you more in ongoing present, heading to the future, snapping away the previous temporary textures. Count on my shades and forget those just the moment you find me as your only one. Then you might come across constant shortcomings I was battling against, question on my personality of moral and practical being. Thus career of destroying encounters, lifestory being heated up under the patience, family to come along with pressure on shoulder to recover, to make it out from my unfinished jobs and to take new responsibilities to settle down for new adventure .Being bullied, being underrated, being mentally tortured, being degraded down, being laughed on, being loser, being broken, being cheater, being great when looking like none. School life of interesting pond while collaborated with college life as the sea of roller coaster of next stage of life.A childhood with many memories, unsung lines and mentioned outcomes, hobbies, aims and daily dramas.An open letter for my someone special, myself ,repeating each word I utter.

Bhaskar Malakar

Dear Someone,

"Whenever I think about your presence my mind almost becomes muddled without words and a heart full of emotions … Still now it's hard to accept all the drastic changes that happened long ago……

I know, I can't see you anymore ………
I know, I can't feel you anymore…………
But, I can't forget you anymore …..

Whenever I feel gloomy, I used to close my eyes and feel the times being with you. Every single time, when I open my eyes it will have a clear perception to face my daily challenges. Re-collecting all those beautiful memories and those heart -whelming encouraging words when you were with me will wake me when no bone is ready to heal me. Even though you are not here you never failed to lift me cheerful. Your courageous words in me have no end.

Almost a decade passed your thoughts keeps me warm and lights up all the darkest phases which I have crossed so far.
Death cannot be the end for any loving souls, when the love and trust in that person fails then it becomes the real death. I know you will be showering all your love and guidance in some other way on me.

Accepting this bitter truth with pain, that I really miss you a lot !"

Your loving,
Danica

Danica Raye

Dear Dev

We had promises to keep; which I seem to have broken.
Promising to love each other forever.
Because now I don't love you. Now I Respect you!
The mistakes I've made are usually termed as sin. Though I have blamed you for being equally at fault.
Who instigated? Who drive me to it?
Doesn't matter. what matters is that I strayed!
Out of our relationship!
All that is done and dusted.
Now what matters is our newfound relationship, where we fight to be equal!
Yes this fight is better than the tolerance that took us away from each other.
You always get frustrated that you don't know my complete past; yes you don't but I'm afraid if you do you'll be more hurt than ever.
So let's cherish the newfound respect and respect our equality.
Let's decide to be with each other on our deathbeds. Would you forgive the past and want to grow old with me?

Your Aasha

Darshna Suraj

To my ex-Sardaarni,

It has been 6 months already - months of battling from the heartaches that cause tears and only tears. A year of making myself believe that one day, one day we will be in each other's arms again.

I know you're happy now, and I know that I have to let you go already. But, I think letting go of someone whom I loved the most is not easy. I can't remember how many attempts did I make just to move one and forget everything. But, every time I take a step forward, there are the memories again trying to pull me back. This rollercoaster of emotions has gone for too long and I need to end it as soon as possible before I can hurt myself over and over again.

You were that upfront when you told me your love for me has turned to gray. Can you blame me for hoping that one day, we'll be in love again the way we were before? I know you have not instructed me to invest everything on this. We both know that we have our own responsibilities in life. But, whole-heartedly I gave much of my time and attention towards you since the beginning, and I am not feeling any regret about that. The happiest and fondest memories we shared are more than important to me.

Those happy memories turned to bad ones. I have to help you adjust on the new step you took in your career path. Not to mention the nights I stayed with you trying to make you feel better because you were so depressed. You then became my only world - the only one I want to be and spend the rest of my life with.

For me, my cellphone became my very best friend next to you, as we constantly exchanged messages 'till our eyes close. I never complained about that. I know deep inside that there was something with those messages that made our relationship grow stronger.

When our text messages and exchange of calls suddenly lessened, it was very clear to me that not everything is falling into its places anymore. And I was right. You told me that you don't know what's gonna happen to us anymore. You were so blunt showing me that you can't feel the pain I was experiencing. From the moment you said you don"t know if you still love me, I knew deep in my heart that our story will soon to end. And it was only tears I gave to you upon seeing you walk away.

Trying to move and forget everything are the hardest thing I can do to stop hurting myself anymore. I could no longer count how many sleepless nights I spent crying and hoping that everything will be fine again. I respect your decision since I knew that part of what's happening is to be blamed on me. I just thought that it is possible to spend my life with you 'till the end. I never saw this coming, and it makes me so sad that it ended this way.

Days passed and my devastated heart begun to heal. I am very much grateful for my family and friends who made me whole again. Letting go is not easy, but I have to do it for myself - to embrace a new beginning. Trying to forget everything is hard, most especially if everytime I look around all I can remember is you and the memories we had. Though it's hard, I came to a realization that everything about us will never be the same again. Very determined to move on, I started a new chapter in my life in unfamiliar places surrounded with unfamiliar people.

I know I said that I will only love you and only you. But, after what happened, i can't say that I can love someone else and trust one. You will always have a special place in my heart. Even though we broke up, I don't want you to be completely deleted in my life. Now, I'm just holding on to the thought that someday we can still end up as good friends. I may be picturing my future with you before, but not anymore. I need to run away from the world we built together and start building new for myself and for my future. I need to keep moving forward. As I let you embrace the chance to be loved again by someone, I will also try to find someone who can love me as much as I love her. I have decided to not to cling on my past anymore, including you. For the meantime, let's just allow ourselves to chase our own dreams and find someone who we can spend the rest of our lives with.

You made me the strongest and mature person than I am before. Our memories will always have their special places in my heart. But, I guess this is the best time to bid my sweetest goodbye to you. Wishing you all the happiness in life. Till we meet again.

Sincerely,

From the guy who had loved you deeply

Deep Thind

To cherished adore,

The galaxy of emotions bursting out as a volcano,this is what I feel for you. I was in search of my PRINCE charming but I got someone who made me feel like PRINCESS. The day I saw you,my stomach was full of butterflies but having a conversation with you was one of the out-of-the-way destinations. I had heard of a saying "good things take time" and even my life got the embrace of hope. He finally paid attention on this incomplete girl.That day was the day of carnival. Now everyday was a celebration and every moment was like the last breath of my life.Understanding was the foundation but distance came as glimpse of pain and sorrow though love was the ray of hope that was amalgamating us like water and milk, indivisible. I don't regret my decision but I just love what I had,this would be forever,so what if that person doesn't exist anymore.

Dipika Gouda

Dipika Gouda

Dear someone
I have a request please dont say no to me. I and many others have failed in small obstacles in life. Yes we have failed and fall but only on obstacles but not in life. We all have emotions we all can shout cry become angry or can become sad , but we can also smile and laugh. We all make make mistakes and we all feel bad about it. Dear someone embrace all emotions weather good or bad. Support in good and bad times help us to move on. I know its not costing anything that is why its easy but difficult. Dear someone we need you to stay with us let the result be a event not the end. You know something a sad mind needs a companion too. I hope you will stand by at all times.

Thanking you

Waiting for you
See you soon

Dr. Tilak Dixit

Dear equality,

I know.I know it. Please don't just crumble this leaf of truth even before I have presented it to you. I know you don't quite like me. I know people like you more than they like me and somewhere I am not quite welcoming of that truth and I shall tell you why. But,you know, I had accepted it. I had accepted it because despite bannering only half of me with so much radicalness and ensconcing only the urgency of that half, you have brought about quite appreciable and admittedly positive changes in the social fabric. I appreciate that you have been so daedal in elucidating that half to the ignorant masses and been instrumental in blowing the winds of reform and reconsideration.

I have always been and I still am in all praises for the spirit of feminism and women empowerment that you have pervasively brought in the society and acted your path in the way of deterging the evils of patriarchy.

But sister, you are yet to learn that you are meant to be more visceral, that your rectitude emphasizes on parity that is derived from all-around, true-sourced political ,social and economic facets. You are to ensure headlong progress,being altruistic to all social inhabitants.Yes, including men too.

Few days ago,I suppose you know, one of our friends from Delhi, a young boy in his twenties was arrested in a rape accusation by his girlfriend who had lodged a complaint against him stating that she had been sedated and then her self, dishonored. I was crestfallen at this news and had my initial thoughts completely bewildered. I could not swallow the fact that such a diligent supporter of ours had acquired such deplorable a visage.

But truth had a verdict else. This morning, the police authorities proved the case as a false rape report. The girlfriend could not digest the man's withdrawal from their relationship and decided for vengeance. I could not believe the even evil devise she made to make the plot seem as genuine. This my dear, came as a bigger blow to me and I went knowing more of these cases.I must say,sister,that the figures quaked my very basis but, more of yours.

Sister equality, there has been an increasing incidence of false rape accusations originating from end of relationships, on the part of the woman that remains unconsented;marriage promises that could not meet their nuptial fate, in the case of which the woman out of vengefulness accuses the man of rape, falsely of course to land him in trouble or to extort money out of him promising to withdraw the charges in lieu of compliance with her monetary 'demand'.It is both a shame and lament to see the USE of such an unfortunate and sinister act,or it's condition to pamper one's own demands. This phenomena is not fantastical but very much real and can be easily ascribed to the misuse of the sympathetic and bargaining position of women in the society. To put it more simply to you, they are exploiting- under the garb of one of your watchwords

-feminism.

As the mental disposition of the society is transforming towards acknowledging the position of women in the society, the several social nuisances they have to encounter and endure at home, workplace, streets and even facilities of public recreation, it has simultaneously endangered men's safety- in terms of legal consideration as well as general public opinions which also acts quite as a drive to the former. On one hand, people are all geared up to establish you in their lives and society by uprooting the norms of patriarchy, yet they seem to be really choosy in it- attaching impractical connotations of machismo and strength to the male personality. "Real men don't cry", "you should work because you are a man", "Gosh! doesn't being a househusband feel offensive?"- why should it? If being a housewife has universal acknowledgement as a designation, being a househusband having even an ounce lower would be a breach of not yours, but in this case, my honour. A wife earning in greater figures than the husband is an applauded materialization of women empowerment,their advancement and progress.Side by side,if one looks down upon the husband for earning less,they challenge me. Directly. I appreciate your fight through feminism to protest for women wearing heels in workplacesto 'suit' their environment regardless of how uncomfortable it renders them,as compared to men. But you depreciate my essence when you mock a man for being short in height. Fat-shaming and body-shaming women is real and disgusting but fat-shaming and body-shaming men by use of "eww"s and "God not him!"s is no work of fiction. While equal pay for equal work is an absolute necessity, deriding men for earning less than their women counterpart is no polite gesture. Although the proportions and percentage of these realities differ greatly, either's urgency over the other is impractical and baloney as both bring down my grace.

Sister, I was made to ensure that you prevail in an utmost convenient and unopinionated society. But it breaks my heart to see the emergence of a parallel bias from you.We have come a long way, eliminating social evils one at a time.We still have miles to cover wherein the balance has to be laid equally on both the wheels- not one be lighter or heavier. We need to effervesce on our principles in a more unbiased approach in either case.

It is my request to you,dear sister, not to invent one-eyed notions and stick to them, labelling yourself as me. I have an identity that I see is a far vision of achievement. Our ways are so much similar,honouring women and crowning them with their deserving value in the society,penalizing all atrocities against these strong souls,raising the bar of safety for them; but in one way,we are much different you see-to ensure that the progress of one does not put at stake,the normalcy of the other and as should the present plight oblige me to say,their safety. Yet we are to achieve our goals for the sake of a harmonious society because neither can function effectively in an abnormality of the other's.

This is not a drill.You and I, together, need to, need to act.

Yours lovingly,

True equality.

Gargi Chatterjee

Dear someone,
There has been no reason for me to believe in love because i never wanted to, for the whole world a simple quite personality who is exceptionally good in maintaining her walls to keep the people out and mostly carried a romantic novel in her bag which no one knew. There was a fantasy of mine which in actually was a contrast to my personality where I also wanted to experience the kind of love they wrote about in novels.

So last winters just to give a shot to try my luck made a profile over tinder. I swear you will find all kinds out there but never your own kind from showoffs to gym freaks, from one night standers to road side Romeo's.

When i came across your profile, to be really honest i just saw your name, height and swiped right and BOOM it's a match. You texted, we talked it was like every other guy making a move. I liked your replies we shifted to Instagram.

Till it was 12:30 am of the first day i told i like you without even thinking what you will think. May be because i had lost many people that even having you for a day and than losing you wouldn't have affected me.

In initial we were a copy of each other our choices matched but as we dig little deeper there were differences which i think makes us distinct from each other and i think its beautiful in its own way. Handling me from slipping over stairs to just listening my rants of mood swings in menstruation. When i cried, you were also having a tear pave its way down your cheek.

The boy you are like whose calls doesn't exceed two minutes now talk for hours, who never knew how to write even a rhyme writes two liners for me.I was never an early bird, you were never a night owl. But now i get up early and you also sleep late.

Me the shameless who really came empty handed on the first date. I still feel guilty for it. To be really honest about me 500 bucks for a coffee is absolutely not my thing i am a quite 10 rupees kinda for a CHAI person. Im not a great fan of Alan walker and Calum Scott but yeah now their songs occupies my playlist. The first song you sent me.

"We all need someone
Who gets you like no one else
Right when you need it the most
We all need a soul to rely on
A shoulder to cry on"

This was the first time i heard Alan walker's song and i heard it N number of times.
You are not my first but i want you to be my last, even if we are not destined to be together I WANT US. I just never wanna become boring for you. Sometimes there are the days when i don't want to talk to anyone but only want to talk to you and only you. You always say me to sleep early but instead of sleeping i write mails, messages and even stupid poems which can only be understood by you.I want to write for you, about you, how cute you look when you sleep, when your hairs fell on your forehead and you adjust them, when you do nothing just smile.
I want to write about us till next sixty years....will you be my soulmate ???

If you ever read this do ping the answer i will wait...but remember i hate late replies.

Love you
Only yours

Harpreet Kaur..

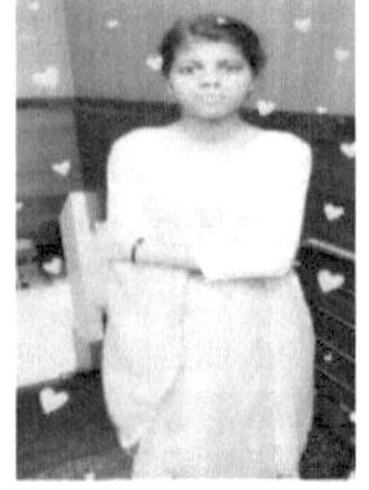

Dear you know who ,
You know something?
There is something I need to tell you .
Something that I have kept it inside me for a long time .
Today I will speak my heart out .
Today I am finally going to say "I love you" .
I love the way you smile .
I love the way you talk to me .
I love everything about you .
You are very special to me .
You remember the time when we used to talk all the time ?
Do you remember the time when we used to talk in between the class
and get caught by teacher while talking ?
Do you remember the time we used to study together and have the time
of our lives?
Those were the times I fell in love with you more .

Ishika Agarwal

Hey,

The day when I am sliding my social media I saw your friend request, I ignored it as I always do. But then also you messaged me ,then we start talking about studies ,career, friendship .
Do u remember ? You asked me why are you so rude to the person who love u ,
Then I opened my broken heart infront you all my feeling about love how I am scared from loving someone and loved by someone..?
I remember you said that if you lost in your first love that doesn't mean life will not give u second chance after sometime I became comfortable with you sharing my secrets with you.
Remember when we met first time you holded my hands while crossing the roads as my father do for me.
From that day I started falling in love with you.
All your silly talks funny jokes shayries ,I just want to hear you everytime you loved me like there is nobody beyond me in this whole world.
But sometimes I behave very bad with you because I am afraid of being broken , I don't want to loose you at any cost because if you will leave me or cheat me I will never be able to love someone for my entire life . I don't have anything except you ...
But thank you so much for loving me that much which I never expected
Love u from my heart soul my love...

Your motki
Ishika

Ishika Agrawal...

Hey self,

This is your 17th birthday and you have lived these years seeing a little bit of the life. A big world is waiting to see you growing but for that you have to focus on what u aim for, not what you like. The world will look as lovely as garden but to make it more beautiful you have to live for yourself and for your dreams.

Firstly I am sorry that you tried so desperately to fix others, when your own hands were shaking. I am sorry that I didn't give you enough time to heal.

Life throws up things so fast that we waste time in deciding which option to go with ,so I want you to be so focused , so regular with your schedule so that anything that comes in your way to destroy you, You can easily live it. The challenges you have gone through, and those you will face in the future may break you down but it will boost your confidence level you will become more vibrant and courageous.

 I want you to be helpful, I want you to be kind, I want you to be loving I want you to face the reality with no watery eyes.

I want you to fall so deeply in love with yourself that you forget what it ever felt like to be hurt by someone else. I completely owe you an apology for not treating you the way you should be treated. I want to tell you your secret, about your magical powers, you have beauty in your hand, you can toil day and night to mould yourself into a worthy human being so don't lose a chance.

Lastly I would always want you to pray to Almighty, sometimes he may not give you what you desire because his plans are beyond our imagination.

Everybody has a darker side, don't ever lose hope.

Jaishi Jaiswa

Dear Leu,

Everything in our life is uncertain. We don't know when and how we have to leave this world. Everything that we will have is our legacy. Sometime it's hard to express some feelings for someone who is very close to you, who isn't expecting you to be so. But you are still in love with them. Life is uncertain, let's confess.

27th December'19. I was excited from the morning. Choosing my dress for the first day, for the day of reception. Which pair of shoes I will wear with which dress and blah blah blah. The more time passed the more I was excited. May be to see you, how much you have grown over the years. Trust me after watching you I didn't recognize. Just assume it to be you. As it was marriage day everyone was busy.Just your parents asked me about my parents whether they will come or not. I was expecting to talk to you but there was no chance. Next day, I mean the day of reception. I came in the morning and was busy in works. I was passing through a mild headache and gradually it became severe. I wanted to talk to you but there were lots of people. And finally at the time of lunch I somehow manage to ask you your name. Next day I was ready to return home. I didn't know when we gonna meet again. So it was important to be in touch. That's why I asked your number. And from there the story begins. I thought you are a girl of least words. But you shocked me with your frankly behavior. Seriously I was impressed. And the conversation goes on.

5th January'20. Today it's been a week since we share our number. I am surprised that one week passed. Don't know how many things we have shared each other about our life, incidents. I have told you everything that happed with me. My downfalls, my ups.

8th January 20. You greeted me in the morning. Everything was normal. Like other days. I was happy. Since you are in touch. And then suddenly you told me about texting less. I was speechless. I was happy because you didn't want to cheat your parents. But I was sad for me. But I know how to manage me. I know to suppress my feelings. I told nothing. As I didn't want any problem with you. At

least not because of me. And on emotions my feelings for you expressed without my concern. I didn't know what I should say, how I should hide my emotions.
I never thought you will ever be mine. You will love me like this. I know sometime I failed to understand you but I am incomplete without you. Thank You for all your love, Care and Support. For being always be there when I needed you most. For understanding me. I love you.
Your,
Chotu

JiaulIslam

Hey Crush,
So its start from 5th May 2018 when I met you dressed in greenish I say blue you say t-shirt and yes those twinnie pants. When I was soo happy to see you and I thought you were there just because of me. The time I spend with you is the best always. You remember that day me and my so called Bestie at the roof top was discussing 'you' instead of life! Yes She gave me the happiest moment of my life saying that you too have a crush on me and I started believing that yes my life is a Fairytale indeed. Days passed and I started becoming close to you but then I got a tight slap at my face when I got to know that she was a lier and she was betraying me,then I started dreaming that 'MY DESTINY BE THE WORST BECAUSE I NEVER GET WHAT I LOVE UTMOST' but then after few days we got to know her reality and I started dating you CRUSH!
Thank you for making me believe that yes EACH AND EVERY DREAM CAN COME TRUE! Thank you for existing my MIRACLE because now I believe that Yes Miracles do exist!
You are and will be the best part of my life from my crush to my eternity our bond just grew deep.
Cheers to the forever we will create

~Someone yours till eternity
LS
with love

Lakshita Shrimali

Oh God,

I pray you daily. I pray to keep everyone happy. I wanted you to protect everybody. Make this world disease free.
Don't make people suffer from illness and pain. Bless all with good water and good oxygen.
See that all the natural resources be available till human races extinct. Don't be partial in making the food available.
Give manageable problems. Test human patience for a level. Make people more involved in thyself.
Make people understand their own *KARMA* , the biggest to understand in life.
Be partial in giving punishment according to karma. My humble request is to tally one's karma in the same life and not to extend to the other Janma.
Fulfill wishes of each and everyone. Bless to live in their own way. Teach lessons as how to live a contented life.
Prove yourself correct. Prove that beyond its benchmark, even Amruth becomes poison.
Be near the person who seeks your help. Take people in your way.
Make them believe that you are the one who give problem as well as its solution.
You show the path in which they should walk. Show the success with and without hurdles.
Remove ego in the minds of people. Remove status gauge in the minds. Teach equal treatment of human .
Preach the importance of loyalty. Kill the thought of enimism.
Inculcate the habit of sharing and caring.
Live and leave others to live should be the motto of life.
Kindness should be the way of approach to people.
No thought should come for lending helping hands.
Teach others and spread knowledge should be the aim of life.

God I have written whatever I wanted to speak with you in person. I thought this would be the best and only way to approach you personally. Let this be with you. Help the world be like how I wished to.

Mahalakshmi Harsha

Hi Dad,

Didn't know that someday I'll be writing something like this to you! U know that I am a very strong and a brave Girl . And Bold enough to Handle the Challenges of My Life. But today I write to you not only as your Daughter but one of many Daughters who know the unique intricacies of the lesson only their father could teach them. You Taught me many lessons about what it means to truly love and experience this Life.

From the time you sent me to the Boarding School , I realised how tough it was for me to not see you by my side when I woke Up. How helpless I felt when There was no one to put up my Tie . And craving for the pampering u did when I got Sick .

And Years Have passed Leaving me back in the same boarding school Where You left me as your little peice of heart to be shaped and Given Shine to. I just wanted to say something and Thank you for what all you have done for me till now.

I remember sitting with you on the front seat of the car and going for my practices . I remember being pampered more than Bhaiya all the time . I remember you brought me gift for every 1st rank I acquired in my class. I remember that you daily called me before coming home from work to ask me what I wanted!! I remember all because it lives in a heart of Daughter Forever what her Father does For Her.

Dad, you were the first man I ever loved. You Held Me , played with me and Supported me and let me Grow. Your patience, quiet notion of complete understanding and unwavering love made me the girl I am today.

You told me that there are things that I can never control, such as how people choose to think and act towards me or about me. So, why worry about these things? Why spend your days frowning because of matters that aren't supposed to be your problems? Why question your greatness just because of other people's failure to see your spark? I remember every bit of words you said and still those fine words echo in my mind.

You said that the blood that's rushing through my veins is the blood of people, of a family, that never gave up. You said that one should never lose sleep when she knows she did her best.
Keeping all you've said In my Heart and moving on in my life facing unexpected realities and Challenges!
Thank you, Thank You, Thank you for shaping me as a Diamond which couldn't break so easily.
I love You Dad.
Often a dependable and trustworthy father figure can become a scarcity today, for I am blessed enough to be graced with one like you, I feel the strength of that presence.

YOUR NOT SO LITTLE DAUGHTER.

Mamta Bhagat

Hey

Two weeks after the 11th classes started, as usual I came to the computer lab, was listening to the class .There was something different.one new face sitting on the last bench was all I noticed. She was silent as a normal newcomer would be. The days passed, she was the same silent, shy and simple. It was the time when she already made a special place in my heart. Few days later it was a C++ programming test, none of could write those long programs except to that shy girl. She was called to the board, made to write the test on the board. She did it as if it was a cup of tea for her. I fell for her that day. Yes, it's weird to fall for a girl because she did best in her test, but this is it.

Days later I was told her name and about her school. At the same days I noticed that she is turning back looking at someone. Then I was informed it was me. As she was shy and silent I had opinion that she won't approach, so I approached her through our common friend. Then there came a day when we accepted each other. My love was true. I had no intentions to play with her feelings or just pass some time neither were hers.

But the trouble starts now. Let me tell you, our religions were different. We were from totally different backgrounds, still we made our long term plans out. We were happy and it was 2+ years together. We were separated by the colleges for our graduations. I had to move to another city. Nothing was changed until the day her father came to know about our relationship. She was beaten. And there were only 2 questions being shouted at her,

"How dare you to love a Muslim guy…?"

"What would society think….?"

Then after that day she was told and made not to communicate with the person she loved.

This is an open letter to the society & every single youngster of the country,

Tell me, did I knew about her name or the religion when I fell in love with her or did I do this intentionally?

Every drop of my boiling blood questions this society…

 Why do you have problem when two families are happy in their own adjustments..?

Why can't you see people of 2 different religions together…?

Why you want to be happy by separating people based on their communities..?

None of our religion teaches us to love only one's own religion people, then who are you...?

To the whole society,

THINK ABOUT

YOUR PART..

MD. SOHAIL RAFIQ

MD. SOHAIL RAFIQ

Dear Best Friend,

Reaching you out through an open letter isn't the smartest thing to do, but you know me, i have never been smart enough. Right? I am actually reaching out through this letter because we hardly have alone time for each other these days to talk in detail and i could not gather enough courage to talk to you in person.

I am really happy that you have found a dating partner, i really am. I know you two are really close and love each other and i love you both as a couple. But you know what? Somehow i feel that we have been distanced from each other. No, i am not complaining to you about this, instead i just want to tell you how i have been feeling these days.

I know you love spending as much time as possible in the day with your love , but i really have been missing you all these days. All of your time before was mine, and now i have to share you. No i am not jealous (or maybe i am). I miss the time we used to spend together, long conversations on phones, naughty pranks we played and YOU!We don't even meet daily these days and when we do you are either with him/her or are in hurry to go meet him/her. I understand that there are only 24 hours in a day and you really want to spend like 20 with him, but hey! Can i get just one hour. Only for us, talking about us. Sometimes, i really want to hear your voice and all i hear is the machined voice saying " the number you are calling to, is speaking to someone else. You can wait or call again later." It really kills me to hear that.just want to tell you that i wrote this letter
To the person who understands me,
who sees the pain behind my smile,
who knows when i am lying.
To the one who has been my crime partner,
the one who has ducked me out of difficult situations,

The one who has sometimes landed me in trouble too.
I wrote this letter to you in the hope,
No not hope but with the belief that you will understand me.

Your BFF

Mohit Birla

Let me love you, till the end of eternity

Dear Crush,
You don't realise you're falling in love until you are
head over heels. I never really believed the truth of this
statement. Until I met you.
I wouldn't say it was love at first sight. Because who
are we kidding? It wasn't. I didn't even like you to begin
with. You were just another person I peacefully coexisted with. We
didn't talk much, just smiled and
nodded at each other awkwardly before one of us left
the room.
One day, we were just sitting in profound silence as
usual, and the next day, I realised I was crazily in love
with you. Did it happen like that? Well, it seems so to
me. But in reality, it took an entire year for me to reach
at this point, where even amidst my grief, the mere
thought of something rather ordinary that you said to
me the other day lights up my whole face in one of the
brightest smiles ever.
From being indifferent to you, I have gone to craving
you. When did this unexpected change happen? Was it
the first time you held my hand when we were crossing
the street and just that simple, warm touch of yours
was enough to send frissons spiralling through my
entire being? Or was it the first time your hair brushed
my temple when you pulled me close and pressed the
side of your face to mine, and every single nerve in my
body turned hypersensitive to that single point of skin
contact between us?
Or maybe it was when you took my hands and shoved
them gently inside the pockets of your hoody, so that
my hands stay warm in the biting cold, and were now..
wrapped tightly around your muscular torso; but the

sensations I was having as if I rode pillion. Oh, honey, they are ineffable. Just the feeling of being pressed so close to you, so intimately – it was enough to warm me up to a hundred degrees even in the zero degrees weather.

Maybe it was the first time you made me laugh with one of those silly jokes of yours. Maybe it was your smile – your full-blown, childlike, winsome smile that displayed all of your pearly whites and made my heart melt into a puddle instantaneously. Ah, that smile! It truly can win over anyone's heart, even my own frosted one. It has to be the most natural, most honest smile I've ever seen. Nothing fake about it.

Maybe it was the first time you wrapped your arms around me and hugged me. I still remember as if it was yesterday. Goosebumps erupted on my skin, which was ironical because your embrace was pure warmth. And somewhere deep within my heart, I felt something I had never ever felt before in anyone's arms except my own mother's. The feeling of being completely secure and content. Like nothing or nobody could ever touch me while I was encircled by those arms. My heart was truly content and at ease for the first time in a long time. I had never felt happier like I had gotten everything I could have ever wished for. My life finally found its meaning, its purpose, and its destination.

I don't know. I cannot pinpoint the exact moment I fell for you. But if I had to make a wild guess, I would say, I fell for you each time you looked at me with that kind, loving eyes, each time you laughed, each time you hugged me, each time we talked. I fell for you every single moment, little by little. All of those moments with you I just mentioned? No single one of them made me fall for you. It was each little moment. It was an

elaborately beautiful collage of those and many, many
more moments with you that led to this – my present
condition. You stole my heart, my breath, my sleep, my
peace. You big thief! But I don't think anyone has ever...
been happier of getting robbed of so many precious
things before.
Yes, you heard it right. I'm happy. I'm completely and
truly happy that I lost my heart to you. And you can
keep it by the way; I have no intention of getting it
back. And while I know I won't be getting your heart in
return for it, it cannot make me regret falling in love
with you. Never. Loving you completes me. So, I'll
continue loving you, exactly like this. No expectations,
no strings attached. Just one request. Please let me
love you. You don't have to love me back, but allow me
to love you from afar. That's all I want this Valentine's Day. The right
to love you till the end of eternity.
Yours and only yours,
Unconditional lover..

MuskanBaheti...

Hey

The day you approached me I thought that it's all fake. Since I don't trust love as per my past experience I thought you will also leave me and go.

But then I got addicted talking to you and I fell in love with you. You made me believe in love again and I started living happily in a dream that this is what I want and this is the end.

But then all of a sudden it happened what we were fearing. We had to end it just because we can't have a perfect ending. You know why? Just because we are from different religions.

This India is known for many cultures and religions but the mentality is that a Hindu can't marry a Muslim. It was because we both need to end up. I still miss the warmth of your arms, the sweetness of your words and the unconditional love you showered daily on me. I was your angel n you were my Mr. Perfect.

But life gives us a set back and today again I fear from the word love. Just miss you and will always wait for him, forever.

Your Angel,

Muskan!

Muskan Sachdeva

Bhagyesh

Simple and sweet boy
Doesn't want to be used as a toy,
Simple being,
Earns for a living,
Quiet and calm,
Who will never harm,
Boy with big dreams,
In future may live with queens,
Knows many instruments,
Doesn't need any influence,
Man with a golden heart,
Knows what he is doing from the start,
Blessed with a happy face,
Doesn't have to struggle for place,
His family is caring,
Who have a lot of daring,
Hopefully he maybe blessed with a good wife,
Who will stand by him all his life.

Nishant Vaidya...

This open letter is for Political/Spiritual/Religious/Social leaders who are in important positions in influential organizations of different levels (global / national / state / district / local).

Dear Sir/Ms,
Political/Religious/Spiritual/Social environment in the country shows the capabilities of the leaders. Unnecessary competitions among these organizations make the country weaker and public bear losses for their differences. How leaders of any organization deal with internal and external differences matters a lot.

Politicians, Spiritual Gurus, Celebrities: people choose them and follow them. If things are not fine; either choice is not right or people are not following correctly. People need to improve their wisdom to get better leaders.

People in public want to be close associates of influential people/celebrities for their personal gains. These kinds of followers/supporters build political pressure on other people in public when their evil plans feel threatened. Does your organization have any policies on how to deal with such followers/supporters?

It is ironic, people want to associate with political/social organization to be known as active social reformers; want to associate with spiritual organizations to be known as wise people. How do your organizations deal with show-off/fake people to maintain high quality output?

How do political organizations take advantage of millions of their supporters to end corruption? How religious/spiritual organizations take benefit of millions of their followers to settle peace?

Political and spiritual organizations have huge impact on other organizations as well e.g. Businesses, service providers, educational institutions. It is not only politicians who play politics, but politics is played inside every organization these days. When corrupt leaders feel threatened, corrupt people/public from various organizations become their shield. How does your organization deal with such people?

Great powers and higher positions come with great responsibility. If powers are misused or not used when required, should powers be taken back or not?

As an individual if I only see weaknesses/mistakes of others and ignore mine, I cannot grow; it is my own loss. It will also impact adversely people around me. Same applies to organizations; political/spiritual organizations must introspect and improve for their own betterment and for the public.

Best Regards,
Pardeep Bogra

Pardeep Bogra

Dear someone!!

When the world shouts that love is all about sacrifices I was totally flabbergasted.

These sacrifice are something like eating your favorite creamstone ice cream with severe toothache or waiting every minute nah nah every second of a day to see your post everyday secretly or seeing all your favorite hero movies whom I hate the most. Are these called sacrifices you really need to tell me the truth. But the thing u need to understand is dear, I am not loosing my taste I am relising your every taste. Those moments fills me with a smile across my face with a tear in my eye.
when I am heartsick I see your pictures, when I am overjoyes I see your pictures it's because of strength u stiched my cold heart with. you are my tornodo of feelings. seeing you from far gives me sparks that light up the imagination of you running towards me with bouquet of tulips.
If love is in the air, I promise you to protect the air from pollution. These letter is not about my love or these love can't be described with this letter. It is a bridge to connect my love with your love.

confessing my love to you is never easy, yet there comes ability to face someday with these letter in your hand and tulips in my hand.

Yours crush
Pavani.

Pavani Vedantham

My soulmate,
It's mandate for you to read my confessing letter, as this letter will convince you of many things.
You are my heart, my soul, my whole world and morsoever you are my life's goal.
Sorry to initiate a fight with you.The more I fight with you and do not talk, the more your place grows in my heart. You are more beautiful than the moon, more precious than the diamond.
You are sweeter than the chocolate and cuter than the infant's smile. The way you smile, the way you look, the way you press your lips, the way you cry for me and the biggest thing the way you love me, I feel my self the luckiest creature, made by god, in this world. Thank you for the late night laughs and the early morning kisses. The way you always want to listen from me the three lovely words, I get myself placed on the throne of Indra. Remembering our first kiss in the late night of rainy season, my heart starts beating for you. Baby, I'm sorry if I'm too stubborn sometimes. Just remember that I'm so much in love with you that I can't see your eyes with tears. Whenever you share your hopes, dreams, problems, happiness and help me to share mine; you touch my heart deeply and I promise, in this heart, there will never be anyone else.
The most important thing, I become butterfly when you smile to see me. I just think about the time when you kiss across my chest, stomach, forehead and take me into your arms tightly, I feel myself in the seventh heaven. But the next moment, your absence makes me cry.
Thank you for being the greatest girl I ever met and being for my life.
Yours Always
Pawan Pratap Singh 'Sameer'

Pawan Pratap Singh

Dear someone,

Hey, how are you? Hope you are doing great! Hope life is going good without my presence in it! Hope you got someone of your type! Hope you are happy in every aspect of life!

I miss you. Yes, I miss you. Every morning, every noon, every evening, every night, every day, every week, every month, every year.

Each second, minute, hour is increasing the distance between us. Distance is playing the supreme role of not seeing each other over years.

Do you remember, when we talked over the phone for the first time? I think hardly the call is going to be 10 mins but when did that 10 minutes turn into 1 and a half hour we both didn't realized. And that one day call became our habit. We talk about the whole world except ourselves. Then, video calls finishes the distance between us by bringing us in front of each other over the phone. We fight, we argued, we cried, we apologized, we laughed, we loved...

Do we still love?

Because this time when I cry, you don't care to pamper me, weeks passes away without any conversation, Relationship feels like burden, more than love we argue and fight.

And then finally one day, you said -

" It's over. Yes, It's over between us"

I cried, I asked why!

You said I am not your type, we can't we happy with each other, I am immature, I belong from a different culture, I am annoying, irritating and you left.

You didn't even turn back to look in what condition I am after hearing this.

My happy world disappeared with a wink of eyes, my smile sinks into the ocean of sadness like the titanic sinks, tears of rain falls down from the clouds of my eyes...

I wanted to scream and say you,

I am not immature. Just because I love you I never said anything to you. If I am an immature, then I would have irritate you by calling daily, doubting on you, fighting with you, and most important by not understanding your past.
But, I did none of this.
I patiently waited that one day everything will become Fine. You will understand me, my little childish behaviour, my romanticism, my heart.
But, I failed. You never understand me.
Hope, someday we both understand each other.
We ended a beautiful story before it begun.

With lots of love yesterday, today and tomorrow
I Love You
And I Miss you

Your's forever
Puchhi

Payal Banerjee

The valentine's week

Dear love,

We know each other since childhood...but never thought that we would ever be together like this. Well , it's been said that whatever happens, happens for the best and you know what you are the best thing happened to me ever.

I know it's difficult for both of us.... definitely it would be because it is a long distance relationship. But then again , the only thing I know is Love and Trust which really matters and I know it's the best thing which we share.

We love each other and we trust each other even more and that is just enough for us to fulfill our relationship with love and loyalty.

Do you remember that day when you came back after soo long but we were not able to meet properly because I had to leave but you took a promise that the next time I had to take you out. And that day came soon and I think that was the best moments created with you.I still remember those insane laughs and beautiful moments we created and captured in pictures. That moments when I had hold your hands and slept on your shoulders.

And do you remember when the time came for us to leave back to home...you stopped me and asked me for 5 mins more to stay back with you. You know that moment I realised that I fell in love with you and I think you too. Our best friendship got converted into relationship and this is it , here we are now , apart from each other but still together in each other's heart.

We live with the feeling of each other's presence around us and our only way to talk are phone calls and vedio calls. I remember when you told that you hate long distance relationships and it would be so tough for us but then thank you because you trusted our bond , our relationship.

I may cry out sometimes , which you hate the most , because I would remember our day , our talks and our laughs. I was incomplete without you , you completed me. You gave me the reason to love myself, to live myself. You became the reason of my smile and today you became my life. I love the way you make me feel special every day , the way you call me yours , the way you look into my eyes and the way you call my name with your surname. Your naughty talks , your silly laughs , your priceless smile and your talkative eyes make me fall in love with you again and again. Remember those ways how we decide and try to be together for our higher studies. Our bond is the special and you are even more special.

Today I write this to you to promise you that I will be yours always and help you fulfill all your dreams. I promise you to be with you in every situation of life and walk along with you in every difficult situation. I promise to make my goal to marry you.

I love you.

Yours favourite,

Poorvi.

Poorvi Kumar

Dear love ,
I fetched for the morning sunshine ,
   longed for a cup of tea;
I drove myself towards the burning ashes,
   and turned towards the deep sea
 I found you in my life , faded ,
 your shadow upon me -
 the deep breathe of air,
and the light of sunshine .
Wish all that comes upon you are blessed with time.
Now with you I'll get my whole life made,
It's the valentine's week, gift you these beauties,
Such roses are blood red !
Happy Rose day beloved ...
Beyond my life, in my dreams, I felt you one day,
In my arms , looking deep into my eyes , you came , straightaway,
Now , I hold you tight, and to you aloud, I say ..
"I love you loads , will you marry me today?"
Happy propose day ..
I felt the cocoa , I felt the dark chocolate,
I felt you , forever, as my soulmate .
Now as I warmly welcome you to my fate ,
Want my teddy tomorrow, please don't be late !
Happy chocolate day my soulmate ...
Brown, black , pink white , whichever you may feel right !
Will bring you the teddy , with whom you can fight .
I'm your waiter , madam , how may I serve ? Will you please,
Help me , together we'll build the temple of love !
Happy teddy day ...
Look into my eyes , promise me darling , we'll stay together , and
forever, we'll sing,
" I've found myself as a human being , under the shadow of your living
 ."
I promise you , I'll be the wine of your winter night ,

I'll never , ever , let you go out of my sight !
Happy promise day ..
It was dark , it was cold , a scene I couldn't behold .
Your soft lips, to me , told , to touch it warmly , my lips fold ;
And , in my arms, your waist , I hold,
We felt warm , though it was cold !
Happy hug day ..
Happy kiss day...
Finally , after I have gifted , proposed , hugged ,and kissed ,
My conscience tells me , something , that I've missed ,
Just , left , to ask you , deep , one question of mine ,
" The girl of my dreams , WILL YOU BE MY VALENTINE ? "
Happy Valentine's Day ...

Pratyasha Chakraborty

Dear someone ,

Tell me something I'never heard before

The tales of those non-existent places ,

The hearts and castles you have conqured , the demons and monsters you've stayed .

Tell me again that the forlorn tree ,

will be surrounded by daffodils

That butterflies will flutter happily again

That rain will dance to the sweetest melody .

Tell me you want me to wait ,

Yes to prove that love works by fate ,

and even if love comes not too late .

I will pray and trust God on what she said you'll be mine someday .

Tell me these nightmares will stop

the scary dreams of me running aimlessly . That I'll able to dream about the greatest ambitions of life .

Tell me that you'll live again

after all these restless nights .

And you won't drop dead ,

leaving the chess puzzles in the midst.

Tell me those sweet nothings ,

that everything will be alright

That after this black winter ,

we'll savour the most bewitching spring.

Tell me you won't get lost in this

abyss of darkness . That you'll light your own torch to get both of us back to where we belong .

Tell me it's a leap of faith ,

we don't even need to haste

our trust and love would stay .

Let them know the power of this poetry, and explore the skies , land and sea ;

tell them to shine bright for darkness to flee.

Prem Kumar

Dear Someone,

What you seek and crave for
Days and Night Altogether In The Muddle Air,
What Dreams You Hold In Your Eyes
The Tantrum Makes It Look Vain
How often you wonder of letting go
Its the Best Time You Push Some More,

You Might Have Heartbreaks
You Might Have tears full of joy
All Full of mixed emotion is what your story of life,

How often the pain you hold within
How Rough Roads You walked through
What is it actually?
These are the moments and These are the Time
All the Blessing you ever count for
Drawing the Best in class,

You Might Seem to draw in the dingy days
When all looks to go wrong
There are some souls who count on you
Make You Belive and Pull you out and Erase them all.

Rahul Tamang

To
The one who couldn't be mine,
And it all was unexpected ,our meeting ,the eye contact ,the connection,
the talks and even my heart falling for you.
How could you start meaning the world to me?
But then how could i not fall for those eyes which tells a lot without
uttering a word,the smile which cures all my pain, and then when you
hold my hand the sensation,with you i felt the way i never felt before.
And i fell for you so unexpectedly
So unknowingly....
i never thought you would had mean so much to me that in trying to love
you , i lost myself and it was only you who discovered me the way am
today
You have become the reason of my smile, reason to hold on things,reason
to why should ilove,reason for whom my heart craves for,reason for why
should i be optimistic and i genuinely love beyond the word love if there
is anything other than that.
You are awesome in every inch if yours,you be the moon to my dark
world which brightens my world,I feel so incomplete without you
because every second that passes reminds me that you are the only thing
that is remaining to make my dreams a reality
It hurts so bad when each passes by without you by my side. My heart
has always been beating for you, there is no light in my world without it
But in return icant force u to love me
I have always prayed for your happiness and well being even if i know
that i am not the one who enlightens your world,who makes you drive
crazy like you make me feel.
I am not the one and maybe i cannot be the one ever.maybeidont deserve
you and maybe destiny wants it in the other way but at least you have a
happy life out there
You are with the one who makes you happy,andi am happy that you are
with the one who is worth your love.If you ever turn around to look my
world and my love, remember that i am not giving up on you i will never
be.
I feel happy to love you,and what if you are not mine, will keep loving
you.
You are my everything, the fragrance to my life, the rainbow to my

sky...and I love you with every inch of me...
I know that I will never have you ,you will never be mine but just
remember there's a girl out there who remembers you in her prayer.

Riya Rashmi Dash

Dear Someone,

A secret love is beautiful, sweet and sacred when it's just a light infatuation; but when that person reaches over and touches you in the heart, making it alive in a way it has never known, that secret love becomes frightening, because you can never make them love you, you would never want to make them love you...but all the same, no matter which way you view it, they don't love you...and your heart doesn't know how to beat the same.

I hid my love in field and town Till een the breeze would knock me down, The bees seemed singing ballads oer, The fly's bass turned a lion's roar; And even silence found a tongue, To haunt me all the summer long; The riddle nature could not prove Was nothing else but secret love.

He wanted her. She'd never tell. Secretly she wanted him as well.

Riyanshi Gupta

My love

As i am writing this today, I have a million thoughts running through my mind. This letter is meant to be a testament to the love I feel for you. A love that is honestly hard to put in words because it is a love that can only be felt. Do you know how much you meant to me? You are the reason I woke up in the morning. You are the person who can put a smile on my face. Even on those days when I am feeling down. You are the reason I am able to lay in bed and fall asleep peacefully. Looking at it, I realise your love has done so much for me in my life. You always understand me and trust me whatever the condition is. I love you so much more than the words will ever be able to express.

I found love and peace in you. I have to admit that it feels scary sometimes because I wonder if this feeling might be taken away from me. This feeling of happiness and comfort in you. It's not your fault. I've grown to be wary of the loves of my life. It's probably one of my flaws in being a lover. But I want to change that. You have given me so much of you, even though sometimes I tell you it doesn't feel enough, but maybe that's not such a bad thing. I'd rather you show me what's real than to say more than what you mean. Or to do more than what you really want to. I love you for your honesty. For never falling short on your promises to me. And even if you did a little, you'd show me that it was a mistake and you work through it with me. I love you for your persistence in this relationship. Even during the times when I feel like giving up (which we both know is often).You always say that I taught you how to love, but the truth is, you showed me how to love. You showed me that love doesn't always feel good, but that doesn't mean it isn't love. You understand this a lot better than me.

You are the one that has reached out and showed me the true meaning of what it feels to be in peace. There is no other person in my life till now who had ever done this to me. You make me feel special. I just want to offer you all the happiness that I could possibly give. I love you and I will always love you. *You are my world,* you are my everything.

I try my hardest to show you my love by taking care of you and doing the things you like. Forgive me if I ever hurt you, or caused you any pain, That was never my intention. I love you forever and always and I will never ever leave you. You are my soulmate, my love, and my best friend. I hope that you and I wil get the chance to spend our lives together because I couldn't imagine spending my life with anyone else other than you.
Again I am sorry if I had ever hurted you and promising you that from today I will not going to do anything that you don't like.

Sakshi Agrawal

Hyy Future Self!!

Well life has been full of love, fun, scary-moments and yaa the overlong nights.

Despite of those unfortunate things and downs [which I am sure, u remember!!] , you've managed to wear sparkle every day and isn't that great??

Admirably, completed the 18 years with the most amazing parents, siblings, cousins & friends and with the experience of these 18 years let me tell you few things-
    1- You don't need a smaller crown.
       You need a man with bigger hands.
    2-Dont hate people.
       Just pretend they are dead.

At last but not least, I pray you have created a life you love. Always remember me, the younger version of you and I hope you are proud of who that was!!

Samriddhi Jaiswal
Dated- 19th February, 2020.

Samriddhi Jaiswal,,,

Dear courtesan,

I know that you had never dreamt of being one, while growing up as a women. It doesn't matter what other's say it is never one's goal to become one.

But, unfortunately we are born in a world where this profession is believed to be inglorious. You are considered to be tainted, and not accepted by the society. You are a women who seems to be a threat to the ' ideal ' concept of women.

You cannot walk down streets without hearing malicious comments on your body , or the work you do. The world around you , have already presumed that a sex worker cannot live like others. They cannot be a wife or a friend, even your families have abandoned you.

The sad part is ,the world is unaware of the circumstances that led you into this profession. The agony you face everyday to keep your clients contented. All the time you need to put on a mask of being gleeful , when in reality you need a break from this life.

The people around you, refuse to acknowledge that you too are human , you too crave for love , you too crave for the feeling of belonging to someone. Someone who would appreciate and understand you, someone who would respect you.

We live in this unfortunate world where you go through hell, just to satisfy a man's hunger but, at the end of the day, it's your fault that you are a sex worker. The public fail to realize that if a man did not ever need to cool down his cravings, there might have been a world where prostitution wouldn't have even existed.

Nonetheless, I am proud of you. I am proud of the women who

looks at her reflection every morning and whispers to be brave . I am proud of women who buries down all her feelings, her sufferings, and carries on with her life. I am proud of the women who has so much to tell, and yet her heart remains unvoiced.

From,
A woman who understands you.

Sanjukta Raychaudhuri 

Dear VIRGINITY ,

People write letters to their pals , colleagues , relatives , siblings , lover , etc ..But here I am a surreal human , writing a letter to you dear "VIRGINITY ". You know what , you are so oblivion of your part in a person's life , especially ' WE GIRLS ' . As we grow up , society starts bombarding us with it's rules and values , and you Virginity , OH MY GOD , we girls need to be so very cautious and careful when it comes to you.

A sort of wrongful mindset is been ingrained within the society that , If a girl is not a" VIRGIN " she is characterless , basically titled as a' SLUT'.
I mean seriously , If this would have been a matter with a boy , it would have never turn out to be an issue .Oh come on , he is a boy it's okay , this would have been everyone's reaction . But a girl , she is also a human being . She has all right and freedom to want , have , do anything she wishes to .

Scientifically , If she's a sports person, she will jump , run , bounce , do vigorous exercise , which will lead to bursting of her hymen and indeed she is no more a ' VIRGIN' ....Then what , its absolutely alright , If a girl isn't a "VIRGIN" . Reasons can vary. Accept her the way she is or just move . OUR VIRGINITY , OUR LIFE .

Yours sincerely ,
Insane friend .

Sayali Wadke

Miss_tbh

Hi Lady,

I know we met recently, but it feels I have known you for eternity. Since the day you walked in, the tables have turned and so was it expected. My uncle while reading my palm during my last relationship suggested a shift in the temporal zones. Glory! He mentioned, shall follow me once the right one has set her foot in. And, it happened. Since then I have not failed to thank you for making me the one I am. People have known me for different but notorious reasons but now they hold a changed perspective.

Do you know how it feels to have experienced the applause from the ones who have cursed earlier? My soul craved serenity, it demanded peace and you came to the rescue. For the one who was distressed, you eased his life. You have made me realized what being blessed feels like. I might love you a little less at times, but respect and gratitude won't be depreciated ever.

I call you "Sunshine", and to be very honest I mean it. I call you "Mirchi" as you have never failed to hit me with the cactus when my work proportions sloped down. You have indeed marked up my success and above that to my surprise and struggle you never have taken aback to make me chase the new heights once I conquer the previous one!

But you never seem to expect anything on the emotional front! How can that be possible? Oh! Yes, you have faced consequences of losing yourself to someone's choices earlier and now safeguard yourself from further pain. Don't worry, I will try to stand by every possible word that I say to you.

Why won't I? I love you! Aren't I supposed to keep in mind that it shall be the ground reason for your father to hand over his "most precious gem" trusting someone to look after her the same way he did? I can't guarantee that I will preserve you always and you won't ever face trouble, hurdles and hard times are a part of being in a relationship and so we shall face it someday! But the only promise I could make at this point is! You won't find yourself standing alone in any situation.

Furthermore, I just want you to understand that I am not in a hurry for anything. I want us to happen, I want us to blend, I want us to shine, I want us to be the one to whom our kids look up to in case they plan to hunt for a relationship!

I demand time and destiny to guide us, I demand almighty help me stand by you by all means. And I pray dawn or dusk, for you to be mine.

With Love,

Your Constant Headache

Shubham Shah

Dear Someone,
I hope you are in the pink of health. I know there are times when we're not in speaking terms,yet the chirpy li'l bird within me never backs off from roasting you with my constant chatters. Even when you decide to snap out of a beautiful conversation and zip up your vocal chords,it's initially a disturbing ordeal. However, my perpetual speaking skills are never truly put down to rest, for, when I address you, I'm also talking to a part of my own. So you who ought to lend me a willing ear! We're complete opposites, with you being the eternal ocean of calmness and at other times, the eerie silence after the storm. And then there's myself, an imperfect kintsugi art at display. But do you realise, my dear friend, that you're but a reflection of my soul. You marvellous-of-a-being who mirrors my sheer existence and yet I always fail to embed you deep inside my consciousness. Physics would aptly term you as the virtual image who couldn't be put down to the mind's screen and the truth reveals the illusion, that is you..! Ah! I am the moon and you're my sun. Even in the darkest of nights, I owe you my otherwise non-existent silver lining. I'd have surely lost my lustre and radiance had it not been for you, my dear. I'm always draped by a blanket of shimmering stars, all represented by countless bodies I see moving around me, yet no one actually reaches out to me. But you do, even it's just for a while! After all how do I blame them?! They're all broken pieces of a jigsaw puzzle, trying to fit themselves into the big picture. They all want to belong to somewhere too,just like the solitary moon. That is why they're busy making their own constellations, their own li'l world in this ever-so-vast universe of ours. Yes, they wouldn't trade this newly found sense of kinhood for the world. Coexisting peacefully,in a perfect state of bliss; such is the fulfillment they have found within themselves with each other's help. And together they shine out to the world, who look upto them with awe. They're so complete, a million tiny dots of happiness bubbling all around me. I try to absorb a part of their joys, but not quite! Oh how I shed those bleeding tears in the dead of the night, hoping to sail through the entire period, trying to survive-gasping for breath! It's only with the first morning rays, symbolic of the warmth you bring in each time you appear. Ah! the faint glimmer of hope you always instill within me...I find all my fears gradually subsiding as all my insecurities are finally lulled to sleep. Isn't that a beautiful conspiracy of the universe?!(**Smiles**) I've grown up in a family that reverred love and taught me to worship the divine love that the almighty bestows upon all of us out here. Some of us are a little too broken, and that's where the light enters. You once asked me how it is like to be in love. Well, love pays a price(after all, as goes the old adage:- no pain, no gain!) One needs to sacrifice a part of oneself in order to experience love wholly i.e to become one. You see, if you carefully analyse the arithmetics, it's always two halves that make a complete whole and there's no other way round to this! Even

Shiva and Shakti gave up a part of themselves while merging to assume the Ardhanarishwara form that we still worship today. Hope you get that someday... Love is the dissolution of the spirit into two bodies and one needs to let go his ego and differences in order to get drenched in the shower of love. I know, your being practical is just not what an overwhelmingly emotional girl like me would be proud of! Probably we all have our soulmates etched out in our destinies and we keep stumbling into various hurdles before actually meeting the"one". Anyway, don't worry too much about all these things. I know you are already battling with your career . Do ace your JEE with flying colours, my well wishes are always there with you. For the time being, I simply want you to relax a bit and savour the taste of the laddoos I sent for you, my sweet ChotaBheem! It's been quite long since I last poured out my heart to you with my endless devotional melodies! Would life grant me just another day to myself? To replay the same episode once again maybe?! I promise you will love my jamming sessions. We'll rush back to the nostalgic 90's yet again, an era where neither of us actually belong and yet our two young hearts find solace in those golden songs of the past. Let's rekindle that spark once again?! Guess what?! I'll make you a nice sketch of your favourite superhero Tony Stark and gift it to you on your twentieth birthday! I wish you would come again another day when we both would be sitting at a Shiva temple discussing philosophy, whispering silent prayers that would resonate with our hearts or maybe discussing the Alchemist at work; simply admiring the creation that is us! I promise we'll walk down the lanes of Varanasi one day,row by the holy Ganges and absorb the eternal traces of beauty surrounding us. I'm ever ready to venture out into the unknown, if my quest ends with you.. Also ,they say that every ending is supposedly a new beginning! Who knows?! All I do know is that this universe which safeguards my dreams and aspirations, rests in lord Shiva's palm. May his will prevail. I'm sure he has planned the very best for us. May he bless you with his divine grace. Do take care please. I miss you.
Love you always and forever more
Yours lovingly
Sreshtha Das :)

Sreshtha Das

Dear Sister,

Just a few days have passed till I returned from a mouth watering trip to Delhi and now I've started missing you more from the core of my heart. When we were relentlessly waiting for our first meet, I didn't know I shall turn out to be a devotee of our love after our meeting. The redolent smell of your hair, lustrous smile, intoxicating body odour and affectionate attitude have me drooled for more of you. When you laugh, it seemingly makes the ambience glow with pearls, when you love, it makes me feel that I'm the only person sent from God to be enthroned the epitome of love and your concerns for me seems more than the entire concern my relatives do.

Maybe my words make me insane or the way I'm expressing my feelings for you seems surreal but it's true I miss us, I miss the bond we made during my 5 days stay in Delhi. You didn't mind my foolish decisions of covering the whole Delhi in just 5 days nevertheless of my work schedule. We had unlimited fun in our hotel from dancing on the crazy numbers , having our first experience of having vodka, attempting crazy things on the floor of receptions and disturbing others by singing loudly. Metro journey was more fun, we planned to randomly hit on some handsome guys, then hit on the cute owner of Spice Bazar near Jama Masjid and succeeded. Oh God! This has some really adorable funs engraved in a short span of time. I'm literally stunned. Our innocent mischievousness got a tag of lifetime experience for me.

I never can think of repaying you the treasure trove you've shared to me because I'm simply impotent to do such. You can't believe how much I daydream of meeting you again and go on a 10day or 2 weeks adventurous trip next. I have more to share, more to show you the affection I've carefully saved for you and reveal all of them in a jiffy.

Besides everything that I mentioned previously in this letter, I also want to convey my concern for your studies. Though I know you're

very much serious about your NEET preparation and turning out to be a nice doctor, I want to suggest you to be prepared with your Plan B in case you don't strive to achieve this goal. I pray to God that you must secure a rank to admit to a medical college, but I also want you not to waste time if you don't make it. Because, your happiness and time matter to me a lot. Moreover, I never want you to dwell in disappointment taking this NEET thing.
Last but not the least, remember in case you need any kind of help in your life, I'm just a call away. Just speak your heart to me not only for our years old relationship but also you take me as your soul sister. I love you my darling. Excited to meet you again soon and can't wait to spend a precious time with you!
Take care and have fun, my love!

Yours forever,
Suchi Didi

Suchismita Ghoshal

AN OPEN LETTER TO MY LOVE

Dear love,
Yes. Yes. I know that when you are reading this letter you will wonder why I wrote this letter to you in this modern world. So, let me make it clear first for you. I have written this because some things are very special and I am not able to tell them so easily. And in any way, it assumes that. The letter has more feelings than any text message. Let's get to the point now. You know what I love you so much. I love you so much as no one else can. You are the one who brought happiness into my life again. You taught me to laugh. You filled my colourless life with thousands of colours of love. You are my world. You don't have to be so happy with the compliments. Alright. I did it just like that. I could see a smile on your face. Which came to your face after reading this. You must be thinking I am not there. So how will I look at you? So listen, I don't have to be there to see you. You are in my heart and every beat of my heart. I can feel you. Well, let's accept it now because of you in my life, my heart is beating. Being with you makes my heart beat faster.
I love you Jaan.
I miss you so much.
Come soon.
Your love is waiting for you.

 Emotional writter
SJ

Surya

To
Rimjhim,

I doog you, I doog you. Do you remember the word doog, the word when 'good' is written in reverse manner? The meaning of good written in Oriya is vaal and in reverse it becomes laav or love in English. So, I often write I doog you. This is my unique style of expressing my love for you. Though at present, I have no rights to pronounce your name, I still can't contain myself. Your red vermilion, red bangles, sacred thread compel me to forget you, but I fail to vanquish myself, you come to my mental horizon, I smile and I cry with you. I am not at all happy with God's decision. The day the echelon separated us, I was unhappy. But the day I came to know that your husband is an oenophile, I couldn't forgive God. The philanderer tortures you everyday, and I am hurt every day. Oh! My Rimjhim, I miss you a lot, I miss you a lot, you are special to me, I am chained, I can't kill that bastard to free you from all burden, my action would only render opportunity to brutal society to poke you with the word 'widow'. Forgive me, forgive me, Oh! My Rimjhim, forgive me, I can't free you, I can't free you.

Yours
Unlucky Manoj

Sushil Kumar Gocchhayat

Dear terrorist ,
You used to call me chessy , you used to call me over romantic ... I
never said a word ;but you never understood it was all love : pure
and eternal, "I love you " may be a mere word for you but for me it
was a forever milestone ,you said that you went on with flow of life
got infatuated with me but have you ever thought about me just for
once,even once .
These all are the complaints to you regarding you because I have no
one to share this pain right now.Remember the secret place where
we planned our first kiss ,which never happened you were my first
love darling! It was an exotic yet depressing rollercoster with you
.its not like that we dont talk anymore, yes we still do but .I just
cant say all these to you.according to you we are just friends or
rather friends with benefits inspite of knowing this intention of
yours I will be there for you.thank you for making me disbelieve in
love...thank you for all the scars and yet "I love you " one more
thing dark complexion never mattered to me because my love for
you was was above everything...

Yours,
Sue.

Sushmita Shaw

The cold wind blows through the lonely night and for the last time
my love I want to give you all □..................... Do you remember
How you promised to call me at 11:59

To wish me sharp at 12□
Just to feel the ebullient smile on my teenage face☺□
How you promised me to get lost in the islands of Tanzania,You
breathing through my restlessness, Playing with my hair.....

How you pampered me to get my favorite kimchi and japchae
Just to glare at my floppy cheeksAnd wipe out the extra saliva
Exchanging an awkward smile...!

Or do you remember the days
When silence used to be our only language
My shimmery eyes needed you to talk to me
You listening to my problems, As if they were lyriced, more
beautifully than the songs of Beethoven!
All of those which sounded nostalgic has become weird for you
now...

You made me love like the strings of guitar
My thoughts were mesmerized by the tunes from your sitar!I've
kept my little memories from the spring
Artfully pressed to melt a stoneking..

Yours words Inspire me everyday to be mature, To build a bridge
from my heart to mind...they say creative journeys never end
Our story is like a lamp that never burns out!

I wrote our first meetings in my storybook..
It still lingers in the sands of my deserted heart

Due to the unwilling misunderstandings that undertook
Your feelings for me long did apart....

Our rare yet precious conversations are irreplaceable
My mood has been left bitter Sweet and lyrical
My childish heart says Thankyou, everyday for making me stand
on our eloped love today..

But!! By touching soul with others, I feel only yours
Longing for wonders to occur and memories to rewind...
Although my sentiments never matched yours
There will never again a story be told as beautiful as ours....

I miss how you held my hand
Lest I should slip away
Into the hollows of lost memory..
My heart longs for all those things to take as replay
For our love story to be much more than just a page summary.

Swarnalata Behera

Dear You,

Yes, You. The one's who's reading this.

You survived. You survived through all the storm that's been going on in your life recently.

I'm writing this letter to no one in particular but to all the people out there who's life has been no less than a mess lately. (*sighs*)

I am an eighteen year old and a depression survivor.

No, not medically treated but yes, I've gone through a lot too. A few months ago, it was like, darkness engulfed me completely.

I was bullied at my high school for being way too skinny. "You look like you're dieting", " Oh no, she's so skinny lol", "she can't do this, skinny people aren't allowed to", etc. I've been hearing things like this all through my adolescence. Yeah, it's true that we go through a lot of changes during this stage of our life but that probably doesn't mean you degrade a person who is not (according to you) "PERFECT".

Step into that person's shoes and try to understand what the person must be going through.

Losing my dad at a very tender age, my mom became the source of strength to me.

Family problems? Yes, I had them as well. I was a very mediocre student throughout my adolescence.

For which, I was taunted. We all have that perfect "Sharma ji ka beta" In our neighborhood, right? With whom we are compared to. I know most of you will be able to relate things at this point of time. No, I'm not bragging about my struggles over here. I'm just trying to give you an example of what the other people are facing nowadays.

The word "depression" Is so common, right? Everyone has this ten letter word at the tip of their tongue.

People fake depression. They do.

You are strong. Don't let anyone dull your personality.

You stand for YOURSELF.

I understand your current situation. I'm with you through out your

journey.
Your survival is commendable!
You've survived on your own all these days. Inspite of all injustices in your life and all suicidal thoughts on your mind, you're ALIVE. You survived today. You'll survive tomorrow.

SwarupaGhatak

To,
Dearest God

I became so religious that only I could pray to you grant me one whom my heart has fallen for. To rise my sun in his colors. The one whom I want to attain day and night for sake of my love.

I don't request for heaven. I just request for my love to be my side. I have heard God has everything so there is no loss for you to give me what I have asked.

You know everything why I called him my forever because with him I felt need for never ending romance.

From starting I used to be your devotee from bottom of my heart now I want you to give my real smile back again in my life.

Stories of ours, of our closeness ,aren't less they are plenty. I miss those moment that always roams in my mind.

There shall be some place in this world where we'll be together. Where only I and him be together with our emotions.

Where the morning will come from rays of his eyelids. And I can hear the lullaby of moon.

I don't know where is this place. And even it exist or not but take me to that place by your magic.

I want to live again and again those intoxication moments. Where I am the sandal and he leaves my fragnance.

I want to drenched together in those rainfalls again. I want to feel your softness and live in those dreams we wove together.

The flame is still ignited inside me that destroys me a little daily in fear of separation from him. I don't want to 'fall in love'. I want to 'rise in love'.

God you are only for namesake if you can't do this for me.

Yours,
Devote

Vaishali Goel